MINIONS PARADISE™

PHIL SAVES THE HOLIDAYS!

Story by Trey King • Art by Ed Miller

(*Inspired by* Minions: Paradise)

LB kids

Minions: Paradise © 2016 Universal Studios. Minions is a trademark and copyright of Universal Studios. Licensed by Universal Studios Licensing LLC.
All rights reserved. In accordance with the U.S. Copyright Act of 1976, the scanning, uploading, and electronic sharing of any part of this book without the permission of the publisher is unlawful piracy and theft of the author's intellectual property. If you would like to use material from the book (other than for review purposes), prior written permission must be obtained by contacting the publisher at permissions@hbgusa.com. Thank you for your support of the author's rights. • Little, Brown and Company • Hachette Book Group • 1290 Avenue of the Americas, New York, NY 10104 • Visit us at lb-kids.com • LB kids is an imprint of Little, Brown and Company. • The LB kids name and logo are trademarks of Hachette Book Group, Inc. • The publisher is not responsible for websites (or their content) that are not owned by the publisher. • First Edition: October 2016 • ISBN 978-0-316-36149-1• 10 9 8 7 6 5 4 3 2 1 • PHX
Printed in the United States of America

minionsparadise.com

It's been a long time since the Minions were stranded on this tropical island.
Luckily, their buddy Phil came up with lots of fun things for them to do.

But lately, the Minions haven't been feeling very happy. They haven't felt like playing mango catch or water-skiing behind alligators or sunbathing in hammocks. They don't even want to have a dance party!

Phil asks around. Why are they so bummed out?

It's December, and the Minions are thinking about the holidays. If they were home, they would be eating gingerbread cookies and candy canes. They would be shopping for presents and caroling.

They would be building snowmen and decorating the tree. And of course, they would be waiting up late to see what Santa Claus brought them!

Phil makes smoothies for his friends. Tropical drinks always cheer them up....

Well, maybe not this time. His buddies aren't in the mood for smoothies. They must *really* be down!

Phil thinks back to how his buddies became stranded here in the first place. He used a little too much suntan lotion,

slipped all over the ship,

slammed into the steering wheel, and caused their cruise ship to crash.

This is all Phil's fault. He feels terrible. He has to fix this!

Phil is full of ideas. He starts writing them down.

Phil makes a list. Now he knows exactly what he
needs to do....Time to get to work!

First, Phil starts making paint. He uses palm leaves to make green paint, coconuts to make white paint, and berries to make red paint.

He paints the sand to look like sugar cookies and gingerbread men. Then he turns bamboo into candy canes.

Then Phil starts sewing some holiday costumes. But who is that Santa outfit for? That's way too big for Phil!

What is Phil whispering to Frankie Fishlips?
Does he have another surprise?

The next morning, Phil only has one thing left to do...climb to the top of Ice Mountain and make it snow!

Phil plans on making the island into a winter wonderland. He can't wait to see the look on his friends' faces when they wake up to a real Christmas!

It's snowing when the Minions wake up! And there's so much to do.
Caroling and building sand-snowmen?! The holidays are really here!
The only thing missing is Santa Claus....

No, wait! Santa Claus is here, too! (Even if it is just
Frankie Fishlips dressed up.)

Phil helps hand out presents to his buddies. It turns out you can have the holidays anywhere you want—as long as you put your mind and heart into it.

It looks like Phil saved the holidays! He's turned a disaster into a party—again! Well done, Phil!